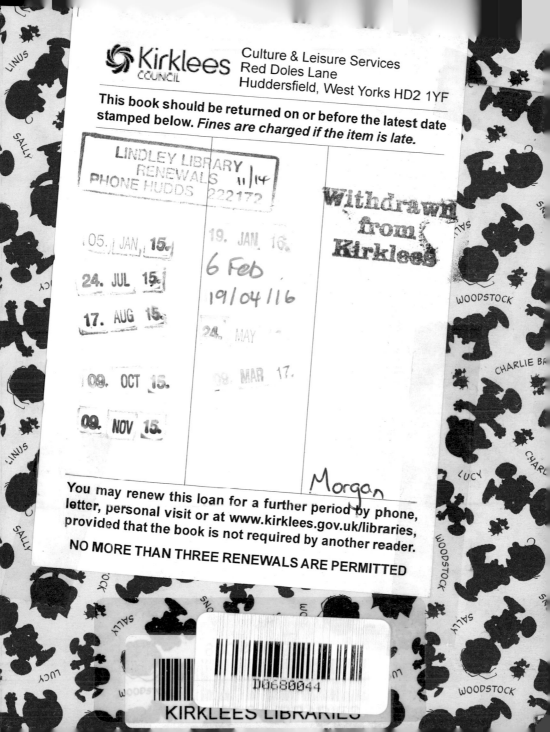

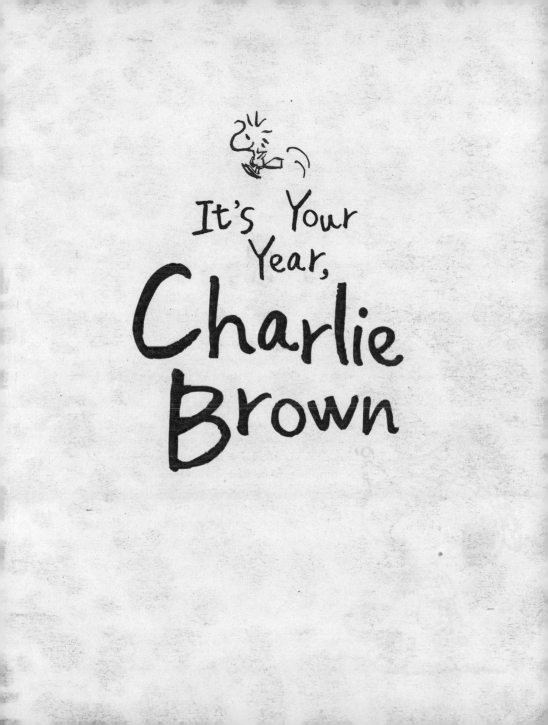

It's Your Year, Charlie Brown

Produced under licence by
Scholastic Children's Books,
Euston House, 24 Eversholt Street,
London NW1 1DB, UK

Peanuts created by Charles M. Schulz
www.peanuts.com
© 2014 Peanuts Worldwide LLC

Written by Sally Morgan

All rights reserved.
Published in the UK by Scholastic Ltd, 2014

ISBN 978 1407 15273 8

Printed and bound in the UK by CPI Group (UK) Ltd. Croydon, CRO 4YY

2 4 6 8 10 9 7 5 3 1

It's Your Year, Charlie Brown

based on the comic strip

PEANUTS

by Charles M. Schulz

CONTENTS

APRIL

55

MAY

69

JUNE

77

JULY

93

AUGUST

117

SEPTEMBER

133

OCTOBER

147

NOVEMBER

157

DECEMBER

173

VERY IMPORTANT THINGS I HAVE LEARNED THIS YEAR

191

December 31st

Dear Journal,

My name is Charlie Brown and I am your new owner. Well, I guess I am your only owner, unless you count the person who picked you up at the store for my Christmas present. I guess they owned you for a while. Oh, and perhaps the store, maybe you belonged to them for a bit, too? And the factory where you were printed? And the tree where the paper came from? *Aaaugh!!* It doesn't matter. You are mine now and I am going to write in you for a whole year. I didn't have a journal last year and I am kind of glad. Let's just say it wasn't a great year for me...

I thought it would be good for me to introduce you to a few people who will probably show up quite a lot this year. It will save me having to explain who everyone is all the time.

Me

Like I said, I'm Charlie Brown, and
I guess you could say I haven't been
the luckiest guy up until now. I like sports.
Baseball is my favourite sport and I play in
a team with my friends. Last season was
pretty tough – we came last in the league
– but I am sure things will change this year. I
like kite flying, although I am not entirely sure why. I like the
idea of kite flying, but so far I haven't had much success at it.

Snoopy

Where do I begin with Snoopy? He's my dog, but he isn't
like any kind of ordinary dog. He's more like a wise older
brother or a teacher I guess. I love hanging out with him but
sometimes I just don't understand him at all! People say a

dog is a man's best friend, and Snoopy can be a great friend but sometimes he can make life real complicated. Whatever else he is, he sure is smart. Sometimes I think he can even read and write.

Sally Brown

Sally is my little sister and she has A LOT of questions, which is kind of frustrating, but can be pretty funny too. She's always trying to steal my bedroom, which is tough to take, and she's in love with my best friend Linus, who she calls 'My Sweet Babboo!' Linus hates it. I'd hate it too, it's a pretty crummy nickname!

Linus Van Pelt

Linus is my best friend. We go on all kinds of adventures together and he is always there for me when I am in a jam. He is really smart and knows a lot about a lot of things. In some ways I look up to Linus, but in others he is kind of a mess. He still has a security blanket. In fact, I would say that even though Linus is my best friend, Linus' blanket is *his* best friend. He takes it everywhere and goes real crazy if anyone tries to take it off him.

Lucy Van Pelt

Lucy is Linus' older sister and is really bossy and kind of crabby too. I'm sure you'll get to see this side of her in action, unless she had some kind of major personality transplant over Christmas. I never quite know where I am with Lucy – sometimes she seems really nice, and then BAM, she'll clobber you with some kind of insult. It's all pretty confusing. The only person she's always nice to is Schroeder – she's head over heels for him but I don't think he cares that much, which has to be kind of hard for her. Lucy reckons that she is going to be President one day, and to be honest I can see why. She's certainly bossy enough!

Schroeder

Schroeder is catcher on our baseball team, and even though he's not exactly ready to go pro, he can be enthusiastic, and sometimes that's all that counts! The main thing you need to

know about Schroeder is that he lives for his music, and is Beethoven's biggest fan. If he could play piano all day and all night I think he'd do it.

Peppermint Patty

Peppermint Patty is a friend of mine from baseball. She is a great pitcher and she strikes me out all the time. Peppermint Patty is good at most sports and picks them up really easily. She is not so good at picking up on other things. Peppermint Patty gets things mixed up A LOT. For instance, no matter how many times I tell her that Snoopy is a dog she seems to think he is a funny-looking kid with a big nose. She also seems to think I don't mind being called 'Chuck'! I hate being called Chuck! Patty is a bit of a tomboy which makes her good fun to hang out with but also means her best friend Marcie calls her 'Sir'!

Marcie

Marcie is Peppermint Patty's best friend and is the total opposite of Patty. Marcie is great at books and learning stuff but really isn't all that interested in sports. In fact I'm not sure she knows the difference between a hockey puck and a baseball.

The Little Red-Haired Girl

I am not sure what to write about her. I don't even know her name, I just know I want to be near her and that I think about her all of the time. Unless of course I am thinking about kite flying or baseball. Sometimes I think about playing baseball or flying kites with her. I hope that she thinks about me, too. What else can I say? She is little and has red hair. This year I am going to tell her how I feel.

JANUARY

January 1st

Happy New Year, Journal!

Here it is – a brand new year with no mistakes in it. This year is going to be my year. I just know it! This is the year the team is going to be top of the league in baseball. I am going to master flying a kite. (I got a new one for Christmas but I am going to save it for the perfect kite-flying day.) This is the year I am going to talk to the Little Red-Haired Girl! This is the year I am not going to be outsmarted by my own dog! This is the year I am going to become popular. This is a year that I will talk about for the rest of my life. The year things changed from 'Oh dear, Charlie Brown', to 'Way to go, Charlie Brown!' I am going to go outside right

now and start my year! I can't wait to tell you all about it.

January 2nd

Bit of a slow start but I am sure things will pick up. Everyone is still on vacation so I have been hanging out with Snoopy. He really isn't so bad sometimes. Still too cold to fly kites, but there is plenty of time.

January 5th

I can't stand it! This is supposed to be the start of a great new year and yet I can't seem to escape the crummy bits of last year. I bumped into Peppermint Patty today and wished her a Happy New Year. She wasn't pleased to see me one bit. She is still mad at me about what happened before the holidays. I mean sometimes you don't want to help a person but then they kind of force you into it. I didn't think it was a good idea to get involved, and it turns out I was right. I got no thanks for my help. I mean, in this case Peppermint Patty didn't thank me because it all went horribly wrong. But I don't think it's fair that I get the blame, especially seeing as I really didn't want to help in the first place. Besides, it's not like hair doesn't grow back all by itself.

It all started just after the lake froze this winter. Peppermint Patty got it into her head that she was going to become a professional figure skater. It was all part of her life plan to play professional baseball in the summer and then skate in ice shows in the winter, which would be pretty cool! The only hitch with this plan was that she couldn't skate ... yet. To teach her, Peppermint Patty had got it into her head that Snoopy was some kind of ice-skating pro. I mentioned that she often gets things muddled up, right? Anyway, Patty learns to skate on the lake with

13

Snoopy barking at her from the bank and she actually gets better. Patty is a total sports nut and it really doesn't take her long to pick things up, but still, I was impressed.

Peppermint Patty got so good that she wanted to enter a competition. She's one of those kids who loves to compete, at everything. Apparently, to enter, Peppermint Patty was going to need a skating dress and so she persuaded Marcie to have a go at making one for her. Marcie told me she really didn't want to. She didn't know the first thing about sewing, but Peppermint Patty can be very persuasive when she wants to be.

Anyway, that's how I got tangled up in it. Marcie makes the dress, but Patty hates it, and I mean really hates it. Peppermint Patty comes over to my house and can't stop crying about how ugly this dress is.

14

I hate seeing people cry, but I'm no whizz at sewing myself, and I don't know what to do to help her. I try to tell her that the dress would be fine, but I know it wouldn't be. It doesn't have arm holes. I am no skating expert but I am sure it is usual to be able to see a skater's arms.

Then the phone rings and it's Marcie and she's in tears too! I thought I was just going to have a quiet evening, and now there are two girls crying and I don't know how to help! I can't stand seeing my friends so upset, it almost makes me wish I knew more about dressmaking. Almost.

Luckily Marcie's mum stepped in and made Peppermint Patty a skating dress covered in sequins. Peppermint Patty lives with her dad. He does the best he can, but I don't think he's exactly a pro at girls' fashion.

Peppermint Patty loved her new dress. It did look pretty okay on her. She tends to dress kind of boyish, but this dress was all girly and she didn't look half bad at all. She was so excited about the dress that decided she needed new haircut to go with it. She asked if my dad could help her out.

I told her that Dad was a barber and pretty much only worked on men's hair, but as I said, Peppermint Patty can be very, very persuasive. I took her along to his shop and introduced Patty as a friend I play baseball with. I realize now I should have said a *girl* friend from the team. Not girlfriend, but girl who is a friend. Anyway, I should have in some way made it clear that Peppermint Patty was a girl and not a boy as my dad clearly thought by the way he cut her hair.

Now Peppermint Patty was really, really mad, and this time she was convinced it was all my fault. I mean I tried to tell her that my dad only cuts men's hair! To be honest, Peppermint Patty's hair would have looked great if she was a boy, but I guess it was a little short for a glamorous figure skater.

Peppermint Patty didn't want to enter looking like a boy in a glittery dress so she bought herself a wig. I'm not sure where exactly she got it from, but the wig looked like it came from some kind of circus. She seemed pleased with it though, so I thought I might be off the hook for a bit.

Peppermint Patty came back from the competition still pretty mad, but she couldn't blame me or Marcie for what went wrong this time. Seems as though Peppermint Patty had misread the competition information. It was a roller-skating competition! She didn't realize until she stepped out onto the rink and started scratching up the floors. As I said, Patty is great at picking up sports but can be a little slow at picking up on other things. I just hope her hair grows back soon so things can get back to normal.

January 8th

Darn that kite-eating tree! I saw it today while I was out with Linus. It's my arch enemy. I lost 24 kites to that tree last year. It ate each and every one of them without leaving so much as a tail. Linus tried to approach it but I pulled him back. It's been a while since anyone fed the tree a kite and I imagine being hungry can make a tree pretty mean. I'm not sure if all my friends believe in the kite-eating tree, but I would like to know how else they would explain how an ordinary kite, flying happily  in the sky, gets tangled in the branches of a mean tree for no reason. And how do they explain what happens when there is no way you can get the kite down so it just hangs there for weeks until suddenly, one day, it's gone? There is only one way to explain it. This tree eats kites.

I know it.

January 10th

Just looked out of my window and I swear there is the perfect kite-flying breeze blowing outside. I'm going to take my new kite out for a spin. It will be pretty cold out, but kite flying is a great way to keep warm!

🐭🐭🐭

BRRRR! Perhaps it was a little too cold for kite flying. I got the kite up in the air, but then it got stuck. It was frozen solid. Going to sit by the fire for a bit to thaw out.

🐭🐭🐭

Going to bed now. I was thinking about today's kite flying and I have decided not to be too depressed about it. It wasn't my fault, or the

kite's. It was the weather. There is plenty of year left for me to master kite flying.

January 23rd

Little sisters can be so peculiar sometimes! Sally is always so full of questions! She came over while I was watching TV to ask me if it was Christmas yet. Can you believe it?

She said she wanted to check because she wanted to make sure that she didn't miss it! Good grief! It was Christmas only a month ago and she has already started to worry that she's going to miss the next one. It's going to be one long year if she is going to carry on like this about every holiday!

FEBRUARY

February 2nd

Took the kite out again today
and saw Linus and Lucy out
building a snowman, but I can't
say they looked too pleased to
see me. It's not my fault they
built their snowman in the way
of my kite! Seems like it's still not
kite-flying weather.

February 13th

Tomorrow is the day! Tomorrow is
Valentine's Day! Maybe this year
will be my year. Maybe this year I'll
get a card. Maybe this year I will get
lots of cards. Maybe I will get a card
from THE LITTLE RED-HAIRED
GIRL. I wouldn't mind not getting

lots of cards if I got one from her. I bet I get one you know. I think about her a lot and I stare at her A LOT. I just know I am going to get one.

February 14th

The mailman came and went and there weren't any cards from the Little Red-Haired Girl. I'm not worried though, maybe she forgot and mailed it a day late. I know I am going

to get one. There were A LOT for Snoopy though. I don't know how that beagle does it.

February 15th

Still no card. I checked twice. Sometimes there can be a letter in your mailbox tucked right at the back and you can't see it, but there wasn't one there. I'm not worried though. Cards can get

lost in the mail. The mailman probably lost it in the bottom of his bag and will bring it tomorrow. I know I am going to get one. If the Little Red-Haired Girl sent a card it will be here tomorrow for sure.

February 16th

Today is the day. The card will definitely come today. I am so excited. The mailman will have been by now, I just need to go and get my card.

I just need to go, open the mailbox, reach in and pick up the card from my beloved Little Red-Haired Girl. I just need to go down the stairs, out the front door to the mailbox. Why can't I move? What if it's not there?

What if I walk down the stairs, open the front door, walk to the mailbox, lift the lid, reach inside and find that there is no card? I can't do it. If there is no card, I won't be able to stand

it. If she sent a card it will definitely be there, and if there is no card it means she didn't send one. If I walk down the stairs, open the front door, walk to the mailbox, reach inside and there is no card it means that the Little Red-Haired Girl DID NOT send me one and does not want me to be her Valentine. I can't stand

that. I just can't stand it. I just won't go. I will just live on not knowing. I can do that.

AAAAUUGH! But what if there is a card and it just sits there forever? What if the Little Red-Haired Girl never finds out I like her, too? AAAAUGH! I can't be that heartless. I know she must have sent me a card. I just need to go down and get it. I must be brave and go and get it. I'm going ...

Well I guess you could say the mailbox
wasn't empty. I went down the stairs, out
of the front door, walked to the mailbox,
lifted the lid and before I could reach in
and get my card, Snoopy popped his beagle
head out and gave me a big kiss. Good grief!

And there was no card from the Little Red-Haired Girl either.

February 25th

Not a lot of people know this about me, but sometimes I can be a really nice guy – too nice. Let me explain.

I took the kite out today because it is finally looking a little like it might be spring. I was walking along, thinking about the perfect spot to set it off, when I saw it again. That darn kite-eating tree. Call me crazy but I started talking to it. I read somewhere that when dealing with an arch enemy it is important to get to know them really, really well. Well, I figured, how else do you get to know something really well without talking to it? Anyway, there I am talking to this tree and I realized it has been a really long winter with no kites for it to eat.

At first I didn't see how this was my problem. I mean, I didn't want to give him any more of my kites. He ate 24 of them last year! I was real mad. I really didn't want to give him my new kite, but then before I knew it I went and did it. Threw my kite right up there. It's not like he wasn't going to take it eventually anyway. See how I mean, sometimes I can be a really nice guy? I just hope the darn tree remembers that the next time I'm out flying.

MARCH

March 3rd

First spring training session today! I can't wait to get started.
I guess it is a little early, but we did so badly last year, I
want to use the extra time to practise our hitting, pitching,
catching, running ... well, everything really. It's my job, as team
manager, to work
the team until they
feel really ready for
the first game of the
season.

Good grief! Sometimes I really do doubt the team's
commitment. It WAS a little cold, but we have got A LOT of
work to do and all they could do was whine. It was just a bit
of snow! I can't stand it! It's like they don't want to win.

<u>March 7th</u>

Snoopy is a great dog, but sometimes he can be hard to be around. Some people think a dog is just an animal that eats and sleeps and does tricks when you want them to. Not Snoopy, he's his own dog, that's for sure. Just ask Linus.

Linus came over this morning to ask Snoopy if he would go with him to the forest by the creek and be his truffle hound. Linus explained that truffles were a rare kind of edible mushroom that sold for hundreds of dollars a pound. This got Snoopy interested so the two of them went off into the woods looking for truffles.

While Snoopy was sniffing around the roots of the tree he signalled to Linus to start digging. Linus was just about to start when he heard a voice saying,

'If you find anything, remember you're digging on our property.'

For a moment Linus thought the voice had come from the tree and it scared him half to death. Linus can be funny that way.

Anyway, it turns out that the voice wasn't coming from the tree at all, but from a girl sitting just behind it. Linus and Snoopy were trespassing on her grandfather's farm.

Linus was so embarrassed and explained that he and Snoopy hadn't trespassed on purpose. They just got carried away looking for truffles and that's when this story gets crazy. It turns out the girl's name is Truffles! Can you believe it? Truffles. She said her Grandfather called her that because she is 'as rare as a truffle.' Well that sealed it for Linus, he came right out and told her it was a cute name. He was in love ... and so was Snoopy. Truffles asked Linus if Snoopy knew any tricks and instead of playing dead or rolling over, Snoopy starts doing coin tricks. Like I said, he's his own dog, and he was out to impress. Right then it starts raining so they run to Truffles' Grandfather's barn to take shelter and Linus says he and Truffles really hit it off.

When the rain stopped, Snoopy and Linus came home and Linus told me all about it. He seems to really like this girl. Snoopy has been acting a little odd, too, but you can never tell with Snoopy.

March 11th

I've decided I need to try something new with the team. The way I see it, it has been a long winter and the team aren't feeling ready for the season because they are so out of shape. We need to get fit and do some real exercise. Push-ups, laps, star jumps, the works. As soon as the team feel their hearts thumping in their chests they will feel that need to win. I just know it.

♟♟♟

Well. That didn't go very well at all. I just don't get my team sometimes. All I did was suggest a bit of exercise and they pelted me with their catcher's mitts! Even Schroeder and he's usually on my side! It's exactly how it was last year. I show up, full of hope, ready to win, ready to do whatever needs to get done and the team just don't care. Why do they even bother to show up at the field? I can't stand it!

March 12th

Linus came over this morning to find Snoopy. I had to tell him
I hadn't seen him. He has been acting funny ever since he got
back from truffle hunting, wandering off for hours, missing

his dinner. Linus confessed that he came over because he really wants to see Truffles again, but that he can't find his way back to her house. He came over to find Snoopy and ask how to get there.

Anyway, not long after, Snoopy comes back and Linus asks Snoopy if he can lead him back to Truffle's place. Instead of trotting off into the woods with Linus like a good dog, he hands Linus a note. It was from Truffles herself! Turns out that Snoopy had already been back and seen Truffles for a romantic picnic! Truffles had sent Snoopy home with a note for Linus. Poor Linus. He looked so sad! I think he must have really liked that girl, and it's got to feel pretty crummy to have a girl you like choose a beagle over you. Snoopy didn't even care. Linus says that Truffles isn't at her grandfather's place anymore and has gone back home. He says he thinks my dog broke up his romance before it even started and that he needs to spend some time away from Snoopy for a while. That's what I mean when I say that Snoopy is sometimes hard to be around – dogs are supposed to be your best friend and help you out, but Snoopy always seems to find a way of stirring up trouble.

March 15th

What did I tell you, Journal? This is going to be my year. This is going to be the year when I play for a winning baseball team. The baseball season hasn't even started yet and it's already starting to happen for me! Marcie called this morning. She said Peppermint Patty asked her to call me because her team, 'The Pelicans', need me. The Pelicans won the league last year and she says they need me to help them win again this year! At first I was confused, I mean I really didn't play very well at all last year. In fact, I barely got a pitch across the plate. I guess she must have seen something else in me

– my determination, my will to win, my sense of team spirit, who knows? One thing I do know is that my team will be heartbroken. They really rely on me as a leader. I feel bad, but all the great ball players have had to make difficult transfers in order to move forward in their careers.

Peppermint Patty wasn't exactly clear about what she wanted me to do in her team. She is a great pitcher herself. Maybe she wants to take a step back and concentrate on managing the team? I'll find out when I show up to practice tomorrow. I can't wait!

March 16th

I can't stand it! Peppermint Patty wants me to be the dumb mascot! She wants me to put on this giant bird costume and run around entertaining the fans that show up to the game. (Her team actually has people that come to the games because they love the team.) *Aaaugh!* I can't believe I fell for it again. This time last year Peppermint Patty said her team needed me to sell popcorn! I don't know what is wrong with me. The worst part of it is that I agreed! I'm wearing the costume right now. Peppermint Patty said this is the best way to get into the role!

🐦🐦🐦

Thinking about it, maybe it won't be so bad. It would be nice to be a part of a winning team and have fans cheering for me. It's not like I enjoy managing the losing side every year. And everyone loves the mascot. And you never know, one day one of their players may get sick or have to miss a game and I will get the chance to prove myself.

☃☃☃

Maybe it isn't such a good idea after all. Marcie and Linus think the whole idea is degrading and that I'm crazy to even consider it. I think they are right. *AAAUGH!!* How do I get myself into these things?

March 17th

Peppermint Patty was really mad. I just couldn't do it. I didn't want to leave her without a mascot, though. She was so pleased to see that the pelican had shown up she was about to give it a big kiss when she pulled off the head to reveal Snoopy! I could have kissed him myself. He can be a real team player sometimes.

<u>March 18th</u>

Going to take the kite out again today. Spring is definitely here now, and there is a great breeze blowing outside. I have a good feeling about flying my kite today. I think I learned so much from all my lost kites last year and after feeding the kite-eating tree just the other day, I feel like he probably owes me one.

✿✿✿

Well, Journal, I didn't even
get my kite off the ground.
There I was, all ready to go, with
a perfect breeze and feeling really
positive (it is important to feel positive
when trying to fly your kite, as
negativity really weighs it down) and
suddenly, out of nowhere, the darn

tree falls over and lands right on top of my kite. I guess when
a tree really wants your kite it will do anything to get it.

I was feeling pretty frustrated but I went right to the store
and bought myself a new kite. There was still a great breeze
and still a chance that I could get a kite in the air. I didn't
want to let what happened stop me feeling positive, you
know? Then I bumped into Lucy. If anyone can stop you
feeling positive, she can. She thinks she knows everything
and it drives me crazy. Anyway, she asked me where I was
going with my new kite. I should have known what was

coming. She had that look she gets that says 'I am going to clobber you, Charlie Brown.' I explained what had happened to my last kite and how I was going to give this one a try. Well, instead of encouraging me, or saying, 'Way to stay positive. Good for you!' she accuses me of cruelty to kites! I'm not sure that is even a thing. If anything kites are cruel to me. Good grief! Either way, any positive feelings I had about flying my kite disappeared, so I took the kite right back to the store I bought it from.

March 19th

Linus has given up his blanket! It might not sound like a big deal, but believe me, it's HUGE. If there is one thing you need to know about Linus it's that he LOVES that blue blanket. He takes it everywhere and now he has given it up. It's like a miracle. He was so excited, and I was really pleased for him. I mean Linus is a really smart guy but it was pretty weird that he was still hanging on to a security blanket. I'm his best friend so I did my best to ignore it, but I'm not sad to see the back of the thing.

He has given it up before, and it's never lasted, but he swears this time it's different. He just woke up and knew that he didn't need it anymore. He is convinced that he can teach other kids not to need their blankets. He thinks it's his 'calling' to help other kids 'free themselves', as he puts it. He is really thinking big. He says he is going to write a book and open up his own clinic. He has already put an ad in the paper. To be honest, I think this might be going a bit far. As I said, he has never managed to truly give it up before, but I really want it to work out for him this time.

March 21st

Linus is still 'blanket-free', as he puts it. He even got an answer to his ad. Some kid called Randolf who also has a blanket problem. He is going over to his place tomorrow. Maybe this time Linus really does have it licked!

March 23rd

So Randolf came over, and let's just say things didn't quite go to plan. It wasn't Linus' fault. He was feeling really positive about the session even though Randolf seemed even more attached to his blanket than Linus ever was. He actually wore the thing over his head so you couldn't see his face. I guess that should have been our first clue. Anyway, Linus starts talking to Randolf about his blanket and how he doesn't really need it. Randolf wasn't so sure, but Linus was really determined. I was really proud of him actually. He explained to Randolf that he just *thought* he needed his blanket, and

that if he could let go
of that thought, he
could let go of the
blanket. Randolf still
wasn't convinced
so Linus decided to
take a more extreme
approach. He explained

to Randolf again that he didn't need the blanket and then

took hold of one corner and pulled, really hard. I thought

Randolf was going to cry or something. I mean I have seen

that happen to Linus enough times to see what it can do to a

kid. But I didn't for a minute expect what actually happened

to happen. You see, it wasn't a frightened little boy called

Randolf under that blanket, it was my love-struck sister,

Sally! She was pretending all along just so she could give

Linus a kiss.

Linus is back with the blanket again. Sally gave him such a

shock I'm not sure he'll ever be able to give it up now. I guess it's true what they say – love can be real cruel sometimes. But I don't think love can ever be as cruel as a sister.

March 27th

Remember when Lucy said I was cruel to kites? Well, I think she is cruel to brothers. She is even worse than Sally! Can you believe she took Linus' blanket? After all that has

happened, too. Well she did. She took his blanket and that's
not even the end of it. She took it and folded it into a kite!
She flew it high up in the air (still a sore point) and then it
disappeared. She said she was just trying to help Linus
get over his blanket problem once and for all, and that she
thought her idea for a cure would be more effective. It was
certainly effective at upsetting Linus. Poor guy! He says he'll
need a new blanket right away.

APRIL

April 1st

Good grief! Lucy Van Pelt has one twisted sense of humour.
There I was in the cafeteria about to take a bite of my tuna
sandwich when she comes up to me and tells me that the
Little Red-Haired Girl wants me to come over and eat lunch
with her. Well, I don't know how I felt about that, but I leapt
up off that bench. I mean I was terrified. What was I going
to say to her? But I knew I wanted to go eat lunch with her
more than anything. The Little Red-Haired Girl wanted ME to
go and eat lunch with HER. WOW!

So I packed up my sandwich and went over to where she
was sitting with her friends. I tried to smile, but my face had

frozen. And then she looked right at me and asked me what I wanted. I was confused, but told her what Lucy had told me and would you believe it, she laughed. Not a mean laugh, at least I hope it wasn't a mean laugh, but then her friends started laughing too. I wanted to think of something smart to say, but my mind was empty. *Aaaaaugh!* I just stood there and when they had stopped laughing I just walked away. And there she was – Lucy. She gave me a big smile and said, 'April Fool!' She really is the worst! I know Lucy thinks I should just get over my shyness and talk to the Little Red-Haired Girl. In fact I think all my friends think that, but they don't understand. My mind goes totally blank when I'm near her, I just like her so much!

I don't think I can go to school again. I definitely can't eat lunch there. I feel sick just thinking about it.

April 3rd

Today is the first game of the season. I am trying to stay
positive. A baseball team needs their manager to believe in
them, especially when nobody else does. Maybe I'm just not
cut out to be manager. So far this season, Lucy has asked to
not have to show up for games and Linus has asked if
his blanket can be on second base. It's not like they're
my star players or anything, but still! The
whole team is in pretty terrible shape. We
can't throw, we can't catch,
we can't run. Linus says
that he doesn't think we
would be ready
even if the
season didn't
start until
November!

BONK!

Linus was wrong. I don't think the team would be ready even if the season didn't start until November 2050! It was awful, just awful. The whole side was struck out in record time. We lost our first game of the season, again! Losing a ball game is like dropping an ice cream cone on the sidewalk. It just lays there, and you know you've dropped it and there's nothing you can do … it's too late.

What's worse is that the team just doesn't care! Lucy actually laughed in my face. She says I look really funny when I'm mad, which just made me even madder. I tried to talk to Snoopy about it, but he just went back to sleep. How can he sleep at a time like this? Linus is my only real friend. He actually loaned me his blanket and I am telling you, right then I needed it, too.

That was just the first game of the season. There are so many more to go. We need to get better, and soon!

April 10th

Sally started bugging me again about whether it was
Christmas yet. It's not even Easter! She said she was
wondering whether it was time for her to hang her stocking
up yet. Then I realized
that I had forgotten
what I was going to
get her for her last
Christmas present: a
calendar! You know,
so she could look for
herself when holidays

such as Christmas and Halloween were coming up. It was a
bit selfish I guess. I only want her to be able to look things up
for herself so that she isn't always bugging me.

Maybe I will pick up a calendar for her at the store tomorrow.

April 11th

I guess there can't be many people who want to buy calendars in April. I found a calendar in the store (there were lots of them) and went to pay for it, but the sales clerk told me I could have it. She even asked whether I knew of anyone else that might want one. I was pretty pleased I can tell you. I guess it pays to do a good deed for someone once in a while. I'm going to give it to Sally later.

☙☙☙

You try and do a nice thing for a person (Sally) and they throw it back in your face! I gave her the calendar and she just stared at it for a while and then went nuts about all the numbers on it. She said I was trying to make her feel stupid by giving her something that was 'so complicated'. IT'S A CALENDAR!!!!! It's not like I was giving her a homework assignment. Good grief! She can be so dramatic sometimes. I

told her to calm down and take a look at
it for a while. I told her it would all start
to make sense if she gave it a chance.
Ha! She came back ten minutes later
telling me that it wasn't complicated after
all – it was stupid! Stupid! She said it was
stupid because, according to her, it didn't
have any 'real words' on it. She doesn't
think anyone has heard of words like
'Feb' or 'Aug' or 'Mon' or 'Fri'. In
fact, she said, she couldn't even read

words like that and how can she read a calendar that doesn't
even have any real words on it? She gave it back and told
me just to tell her when Christmas was coming! I guess I am
going to have to put up with her bugging me about Halloween
in June and Easter in October!

At least I didn't have to pay for the calendar.

April 15th

I have been thinking about the Little Red-Haired Girl. I saw her again the other day. I don't know what it is about her but I just want to be close to her. She is so pretty and smart. I wonder if she thinks about me sometimes, too. If she does think of me, what does she think? I think we could have a great life together or at least hold hands or something. I

don't know what it is about her but whenever I am not with her, I can think of a thousand things to say to her, then when I see her I can't think of anything. My mouth dries up and I feel like my tongue has tied itself into a knot.

Even Linus is sick of me talking about her all the time. He thinks that I should just talk *to* her instead. Ha!

Like it's that easy? I'd like to see him try and talk when his mouth is totally dry and his tongue is in a knot. I'd really like to see it, because it is impossible. I should know.

April 27th

Okay, so maybe I should have called today's game. I really didn't think it was raining all that hard, you know? I just get so sick of the team being so ready to throw in the towel. (Ha! I could have used one). I mean the only reason Lucy wanted to call the game was because the rain was getting her cake wet! Why was she even eating cake in the middle of a baseball game? Good grief!

Anyway, the game was called. The rain really started coming down hard. I should have gone home, but I just stood there, you know, thinking about the game. I figured I might as well stay there until the rain stopped. I don't really mind getting wet, you know? I kind of hoped everyone would come back and that we would start playing again. I was pitching a great inning! Well, a good inning, but the rain kept falling. I've never seen it rain like that before. I should have gone home when I saw that the pitch was flooding, but I was on the pitcher's mound. I figured the pitcher's mound was the highest point and so was the safest place for me to be in a flood. It just kept raining and the water kept rising and by the time I realized that I really should have gone home and that I might need some assistance, there was no one left on the pitch to help me!

I swear, I thought the water was going to sweep me out to sea. Linus told me later that there was no way I would have made it to the sea. He was right. The water only swept me as far as the alley behind the supermarket. I landed on a pile of boxes. I was so relieved that I rushed home right away. I was sure Snoopy and Sally would have been really worried when I hadn't come home.

***

Ha! Some sister Sally is. All she was worried about was the fact that now I was home, I would want my room back! It turns out she, Linus and Snoopy had watched me on the mound as the water rose and swept me away. She thought I had been taken out to sea, too, but rather than get help, she got her stuff and moved it right into my room! You've got to admire her boldness I suppose. Good grief!

MAY

May 5th

I was about to write that a 'weird thing' happened today, but I guess when it comes to Snoopy it was kind of ordinary. I mean, it would be weird if anyone else's dog joined the Beagle Scouts and dressed himself up in the funny uniform, but for Snoopy it is just an average day. I'm pleased for him. Perhaps this will teach him to be less lazy and more obedient. Beagle Scouts are supposed to be dutiful and adventurous. He went out on an expedition into the woods and seemed really excited. I hope it goes well for him.

May 6th

Snoopy went out yesterday and still isn't home. I hope he
was a good Beagle Scout and found himself somewhere safe
to camp last night. I bet you he got carried away and is lost
somewhere. He always takes things too far. I hope he's okay.
I'm a bit worried about him, actually. I should have known this
was going to be trouble.

Lucy came over again. I told her I was worried about Snoopy. She wasn't exactly helpful. She said that if he was able to get himself into these scrapes, then he could get himself out of them. In a weird way that's almost a compliment from Lucy – she'd never outright call Snoopy smart, but that was pretty close. It didn't make me feel any better though. I wish he'd just come home.

May 7th

Well that was embarrassing. A Girl Scout called Loretta came to the door with Snoopy! He had got lost after all. She found him wandering around in the woods looking terrified. Lucy is going to love this. I thanked Loretta for bringing him home; it was really good of her. Of course she didn't leave without billing me for all the Girl Scout Cookies Snoopy had eaten on the way.

I should have known. Girl Scouts are always looking for an

easy customer, and a lost beagle is quite possibly the easiest customer ever.

Lucy came over and she was just as you would expect her to be. She laughed at Snoopy, and at me for having so little control over my dog. I'd like to see her try controlling him! Snoopy didn't seem to care. I was embarrassed that Snoopy had to be rescued by a Girl Scout, but I was proud of how he dealt with Lucy. I wish I could act like that when she was yelling at me. Calm under pressure. Maybe he really is a good Beagle Scout after all.

May 15th

Sally may be my little sister and have some pretty wild ideas about things, but she can be real smart sometimes. She has found a way to apply NOT to go to camp. Can you believe that? You can actually apply not to go. I HATED camp last year – sleeping in tents, hiking, swimming in the camp lake and camp food. Yuck! Sally, Linus and I all applied not to go. I hope they accept my application. It would make my summer if I didn't have to go to camp. Imagine, the whole summer at home!

May 25th

Sally and Linus have both heard back from camp and they don't have to go this year! I hope that means I don't have to go either. I can't see why they would let them get out of it and not me. The whole summer at home! I can't wait to get my reply.

May 26th

I have to go to camp.

I heard back today and they have rejected my application to get out of going. Just my luck. Linus and Sally have the whole summer at home and I am going away. I can't stand it! I just can't stand it!

JUNE

June 5th

There's a moving truck! There's a moving truck on our street and it is parked right outside the Little Red-Haired Girl's house! I feel sick. I was just in the yard with Linus when he spotted it. I can't stand it! All of my hopes, all of my dreams are being packed inside that moving truck and going to who knows where. Linus says I have to do something, that I should speak to her or say goodbye or something. HOW CAN I SAY GOODBYE TO SOMEONE I NEVER REALLY SAID HELLO TO? *AAAAUGH!* She is going to move away and I will never have said one intelligent thing to her. How can I let her move away without even telling her how I feel? Or finding out how she feels? What can I do?

I thought I had plenty of time to get around to speaking to her, but now I just have today and that's it for the rest of my life. That's not enough time.

I didn't even get any warning. How am I supposed to come up with something to say to her that introduces myself, tells her how I feel and how long I have felt that way, that sums up everything I have wanted to say to her in the past but never found the words, that gives her no choice but to feel the same way about me? How am I supposed to come up with something that says all of those things in one single day? *AAAAUGH!* I can't stand it! It's too much pressure. I just want to hide up here in my room and pretend it isn't happening, but

Linus is downstairs watching the truck. I guess I'd better go down. This may turn out to be the worst day in my entire life.

❦❦❦

She's gone.

June 7th

The Little Red-Haired Girl has gone and Linus and I just stood there and watched. I watched the movers pack all of her things into the truck and then watched as she climbed into her car and then watched as it drove away. I did nothing. I didn't say a single word to her. I just watched and as she left I felt like she had packed away my whole life, my whole future into the back of her car and taken it with her. I just stood there and watched.

Maybe that is just how my life is going to go from now on. Maybe I should stop trying to fight it. I am just going to stand there and watch as it all passes me by. I'm not angry about it, I'm just really sad. Linus on the other hand was madder than I have ever seen him. Madder even than

when someone takes his blanket. He couldn't believe I just stood there and watched. He said he has listened and listened to me talk about her for years and he can't believe I just stood there. What could I say to him? I couldn't believe it either.

I stood there, staring at her driveway, all night. I don't know why. I don't know what I thought would happen. I just couldn't move. I had just watched my one chance at being happy drive away. I guess I wasn't ready to walk away from that chance. What if she had forgotten something and had to come back to get it? What if a few miles down the road she realized that she needed to tell me something? What if ... *AAAAUGH!* I don't know. I just stood there all night and she didn't come back. I stood there until Linus came back and gave me a sharp kick in the pants. I guess he was still mad.

June 15th

Sorry I haven't written in a while. I have been kind of moping around after the Little Red-Haired Girl left. I couldn't really think of anything to write. I am starting to feel a bit better now though. There is still A LOT of year left and there were so many other things I wanted to achieve and haven't yet. I still need to master kite flying. I need to sort out the baseball team. The season is in full swing and I'll be honest, so far we aren't doing much better than we did last year. Also camp is coming up. I know I was kind of depressed about having to go when both Sally and Linus managed to worm their way out of it, but now I am thinking that maybe it is just what I need. You know, a change of scene. Some time away from it all. I guess you could say I am trying to make the best of it and stay positive.

I have decided to throw myself into the rest of this year's goals to help me forget the big one that I missed. You never know, maybe one day she will move back and, if she does, I don't want her to find that same old Charlie Brown that just stood on the driveway and watched her leave.

I want her to see a new, kite-flying, baseball-winning, life-grabbing, super-popular Charlie Brown. The kind of guy that she just can't help but want to get to know. It could happen right, Journal? I can be that Charlie Brown and she could come back?

June 16th

Didn't I tell you, Journal? Didn't I say
I just needed to stay positive? Well I
did and now something amazing has
happened. At the start of this season
I gave Snoopy a chance to play on
our baseball team. Well, I didn't think it

would do any harm. Last year we did so badly, having a beagle
on our team couldn't make things any worse. Anyway, turns
out it was a really smart thing to do. Snoopy has been made
rookie of the year! A rookie is a player in their first year of a
new sport, and this is Snoopy's first year playing baseball. I
am so proud of him. To think, a beagle of mine, a player on my
baseball team, voted rookie of the year. I can't wait to tell the
rest of the team.

I'll be honest. I was expecting the team to be a bit more excited when I told them. Especially when I showed them the trophy. Snoopy plays for us and he has been voted the best new player of the year! That means we can't be so bad after all. Everyone just seemed surprised. I guess Snoopy does miss a lot of catches, and he does like to take a nap on the field now and then. Actually he kind of drives me crazy, but he was voted best new player and he plays for our team. No matter which way you look at it, this is a good thing. Things are looking up!

June 18th

Oh, Journal! I think I may have finally lost it this time. It all started yesterday morning. I woke up to the sun streaming in the window, but when I looked out of the window, instead of the sun, I saw a bright glowing baseball! I mean I know it was the sun, but I swear it looked just like a baseball. I think the stress of the team and the Little Red-Haired Girl leaving has got to me. I told Linus about it and mentioned that my head also felt itchy. He took a look and said my head had a rash that made it look just like a baseball! He told me to get to the doctors. I get the bus to camp in two days. I made an appointment for tomorrow. I just hope he can give me something to clear it up in time. Until then I am going to wear a paper bag over my head.

June 19th

I saw the doctor and he actually prescribed camp! He thinks the change of scene will do me good. If the stress is getting to me, getting away from it will be the best medicine. Is he crazy? Since when has camp been an escape from stress? I've always thought of it like a journey into it, especially with a gross rash all over your head. What could be more stressful than meeting a whole bunch of strangers, with a gross-looking rash on your head? Camp kids are mean enough at the best of times, but having a huge rash is like jumping into shark-infested waters wearing a pair of meat pants. They will eat me alive! It's worse than wetting the bed on your first night or calling your camp counsellor 'Mummy!' I can't stand it! My positive thinking is really taking a hit. I'm going to keep this paper bag on my head until camp is over or the rash is gone, whichever comes first.

June 23rd

Sorry I haven't written in a while, everything always happens so fast at camp that I never know what's going on. All I can say is that whatever is happening here is good. The doctor was right. Camp is the best medicine! I'm Camp President!

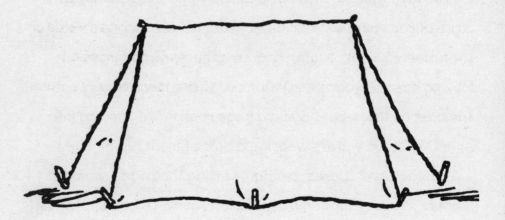

There I was, sitting in the first meeting at camp and some kid says, 'I've got a great idea ... let's nominate the kid here with the sack over his head!' and before I knew it, there I am. Charlie Brown: Camp President. Not that anybody knows that my name is Charlie Brown. For some reason everyone calls me Mr Sack, but I don't think that matters one bit. It's me they voted Camp President, and that's not all. It's like I'm a different person here. I'm really, really popular. My fellow campers listen to everything I say, they think I am wise. They come and find me when they need advice. They think everything is better here since I was put in charge! It is so different to being at home. I don't think I ever want to leave. I'm telling you, that doctor knew what he was talking about. This camp is the best thing that ever happened to me. To think I applied not to come!

JULY

July 4th

It's over – my presidency, my popularity, all of it – all because
I took off the dumb bag.

I woke up this morning and my head
didn't itch anymore. It was such
a relief. I wasn't sure whether or
not I should take my paper bag off and take a look, I mean,
what if somebody saw me and didn't want me to be President
anymore? But I figured, what was I going to do? Walk around
with a paper bag on my head for the rest of my life? I had
to give it a chance, so I took it off. It felt so good, feeling
the air on my face again. It felt so good until it didn't. One of
my fellow campers saw me without my paper bag and any
popularity or wisdom he had seen in me disappeared. I guess
it couldn't last forever, though I kind of wish it had. At least I
get to go home soon. I hate being that nobody who used to be
a somebody. It's the only thing worse than being a nobody.

At least before, when I was a nobody, I didn't know what it felt like to be a somebody. Good grief!

July 7th

It's so good to be home. It was almost worth going away just to appreciate being home so much. My own bed, real friends, even Snoopy was pleased to see me. It's hard not to feel good right now. I don't have to go back to camp for a whole year! In fact I have a whole year to work on not having to go next year. I feel like a brand new Charlie Brown. And that's not all. I came home to a pile of letters from Peppermint Patty. She and Marcie left for camp the week before I did. I know you shouldn't feel happy when other people are unhappy, but it sounds like the girls aren't having such a great time at camp either. I sure wish she would stop calling me Chuck though!

Hey Chuck,

Hope you had a great time at camp! I know you don't like camp very much, Chuck. I usually love camp. What's not to love? No school, lots of fresh air, great food, swimming in lakes and loads of new campers to meet. And the sports, Chuck! You can play any sport you like, from the moment you wake up, until you go to bed. I had such a blast last year, Chuck. I was really excited this year. I really was! That's why I'm so disappointed, Chuck. I guess things get complicated as we get older, don't they, Chuck?

It all started on the bus. It's a long drive to camp, Chuck. I like to get in some sleep so that I have maximum energy for when I arrive. Everything always moves so fast at camp that I like to be ready the moment I step off the bus. No such luck this year, Chuck. Some kid sitting behind Marcie kept calling her names. It was driving her crazy. I offered to punch him for her when we got to camp, but there was no need. Marcie whacked him with her first-aid kit. Can you believe that, Chuck? Marcie, hitting a kid with a first-aid kit! I guess getting out into nature really can bring a kid out of herself.

Marcie couldn't have hit him hard enough though. The dumb kid kept doing it. Marcie had to go hungry because she was so mad that she threw her dinner at him. I felt bad for her. I love the food at camp, Chuck. The other kids whine about it, but I think it's just great. I better go now, Chuck. I heard the bell for the first-night campfire and I would hate to miss it.

Hope you are having a good summer, Chuck! Write soon!

Peppermint Patty

Hey Chuck,

How are things? How is your team doing this season? The one thing I miss when at camp is my team.

You will be pleased to hear camp is getting a bit better. At least it is for me, Chuck. I love being in the outdoors, sharing a cabin with all my new friends. It really is the life, Chuck. I'll never understand why you don't like it, Chuck. I don't think Marcie is having such a swell time though, Chuck. That kid just won't let up calling her names.

I have to give it to him, Chuck, this kid has got some staying power! So far she has pushed him off the dock into the lake and shoved him into poison oak! Poor dumb kid can't stop scratching. She hurt him so bad that he spent half the day with the camp doc, Chuck. I think he is having an even worse time at camp than you did.

Write soon!

Peppermint Patty

Hey Chuck,

I know I am writing again real soon, Chuck, but I had to tell someone. You will never guess what that dumb kid was calling Marcie. He was calling her 'Lambcake', Chuck. 'Lambcake'? I don't see what is so bad about being called 'Lambcake', but what do I know? It turns out that this kid thinks he is in love with Marcie. I tried to tell her that you can't keep pounding a person just because they think they are in love with you, but she said that you can if you think they are being SARCASTIC?! I don't understand her at all. I think I would like it if someone wanted to call me 'Lambcake', Chuck. Do you think you would ever call anyone 'Lambcake', Chuck?

Anyway, she said that she thinks you need to have had a cat or a horse, or at least some sort of pet, before you are ready for a boyfriend. Do you think you need to have had a pet before you have a ~~boyfriend~~ girlfriend, Chuck? I've never had a pet, Chuck? Do you think that means I will never have a boyfriend, Chuck? I guess you have Snoopy so you are ready whenever you like. That's good for you isn't it, Chuck?

I guess I don't understand love, Chuck. Take this dumb kid, for example. One minute he was a normal camper and the next minute he falls in love and keeps getting hit in the face.

I don't know if I ever want to fall in love if it means I get hit in face all the time Chuck? Do you? Do you want to fall in love if it means you get hit in the face, Chuck?

Don't worry about writing back. We get the bus home tomorrow so I'm sure I'll see you soon.

Peppermint Patty

I guess my time at camp wasn't so bad after all. Good grief!

July 9th

I think one of the reasons I don't like camp is all of the new people you meet there. Peppermint Patty calls them new friends. I always find that 'new people' turn out to be exactly the same as all the 'old people' I know. Take the party I went to tonight. It was full of new people and it was horrible. I don't know when it started to go wrong, but it could have

been when I fell into the paddling pool. Anyway, I was so embarrassed I came straight home. I left Snoopy there. He was having a good time. I told Sally about it and she was really sweet. She can be an okay sister sometimes. As I got up to go inside she saw I had a note pinned to my back.

> 'You didn't see me but
> I was the one who hurt
> your feelings at the party.
> Please call me 762-6414.'

So I called the number and it was a GIRL! She wanted me to go over to her house so that she could apologize in person. How sweet is that? Maybe the party wasn't so bad after all.

✿✿✿

I can't stand it! I went to the girl's house. I was so nervous,

I didn't know how I was going to be able to walk up the steps and ring the doorbell. When I got there I wanted to turn around and run all the way home. Now I wish that I had! It was that Girl Scout, Loretta – the same one that rescued Snoopy from his Beagle Scout expedition! Good grief. The minute she saw me at the door she tried to sell me more of her dumb cookies. I'm telling you. Girl Scouts will do anything to make a sale. Turns out she and Snoopy have been friends for a while. I have a feeling it was all his idea. He planned it all just because he wanted me to buy him more cookies! I guess loyalty isn't covered in the Beagle Scout handbook.

July 12th

Another game today – we didn't play our best, but it was nice to see a bit more enthusiasm among the players. I like to have a lot of chatter on the field. You know, the team calling out to one another to help put the other side off their swing. Even Lucy was calling out a few things, but then she came over to ask what else she should say. I gave her a few good calls, but she said it would help if I wrote them down. I was really glad that Lucy was showing an interest. She is so crabby most of the time and she is a terrible player. I really wanted to help her out when she was going to try to support the team. I grabbed a pencil and jotted down the first calls that came into my head and gave them to her.

THROW IT BY 'IM PITCHER!

She started out just fine. It was nice to hear her and feel that finally the team were looking out for one another. Only problem was she was concentrating so much on reading that she didn't see the ball that was headed right to her. It should have been a really easy catch, too. I guess you can't have everything.

July 14th

I'm going to take Snoopy down for a walk by the lake today. I
think it will be fun. I feel like we haven't done that much dog-
and-owner stuff lately. He tends to look after himself most
of the time, but I watched this movie that had a boy and a dog
in it. The boy threw this stick into the lake for his dog and the
dog ran into the lake after it to bring the stick back to the
boy. The dog seemed to love it and
the boy looked pretty happy, too.

When we got
to the lake, that
crazy beagle picked
up a stick and threw it into the lake. He wanted me to go and
get it! Either I don't have the right kind of dog or I watched
the wrong kind of movie. Good grief!

July 19th

I can't stand it! We lost another game today and I swear it
was all Lucy's fault! I don't know why she even shows up. I
think it's only so she can get close to Schroeder, who she
really seems to have a big crush on. I really only keep her on
the team because she is Linus' big sister, that and I'm a little
bit scared of her, but I'm not sure they are good enough
reasons anymore. I have to think of the rest of the team.
Maybe writing a list of pros and cons will help.

Pros for keeping Lucy Van Pelt on the team	Cons for keeping Lucy Van Pelt on the team
She is Linus' big sister	She can't catch
I'm terrified of her	She can't throw
She is in love with Schroeder, and being in love is really hard	She is awful at the bat
	She is lazy
	She makes constant excuses
	She is ALWAYS complaining
	She doesn't care about the team

AAAAUGH! I should have written a list of pros and cons about whether I should write this dumb list. Now I am going to have to tell her she can't play on the team anymore. Good grief!

July 21st

I don't know why nobody ever says, 'You know what, you are a nice guy, Charlie Brown', because I am. I gave Lucy one last chance and wouldn't you know it, she played even worse than normal. She spent most of the time following Schroeder round the field, and he kept trying to move away from her. She missed every ball that was headed right to her, and she threw Schroeder off his game, too. I felt bad and all, but there was nothing else for it – I had to tell her that I didn't think she was good enough for the team.

I'd really like to be able to say that she took it well. But she didn't. She said that if I kicked her off the team she would never speak to me ever again. For a moment I thought about getting out my list and adding in another reason why kicking Lucy off the team was a really great idea, but then she said that she would yell at me at all the time instead.

I still think I have done the right thing. The team will play better without her and all of her negativity and crabbiness. Getting rid of her might possibly be the best decision I have made as manager this season.

July 30th

Tell me, Journal, why do none of my plans work out for the best? Lucy might not be on the team anymore, but she's still coming to every game. Now she just yells mean things to us from the edge of the field. It's really distracting!

AUGUST

August 3rd

She did it. Lucy ruined the whole season and she wasn't even
on the field. We were up. We could have won the lousy game
and made sure that we didn't finish in last place like we did
last year. WE COULD HAVE FINALLY WON A GAME! I can't
stand it!

We just needed to get the last player out. My heart dropped
when he hit my pitch, but the ball flew really high and Snoopy
was right under it. He had it. He
had it and we were going to win
the game!

Then I heard Lucy. Then Snoopy
heard her. Yelling something about
Snoopy having a big nose. Poor
beagle lost his concentration and
ball landed right on his head. Not

only did she lose us the game, but also she injured the rookie of the year; my star player! I had to take him to the vet, the poor guy.

So the team will come last again.

After it happened I saw her staring at Schroeder with a really sad look on her face. I guess taking her off the team has hit her pretty hard as she can't spend time with him. Thinking about that makes me feel pretty guilty. *AAUGH!* It's official. Lucy Van Pelt: can't play baseball with her, can't play baseball without her.

August 10th

I've really done it now! I hit Lucy right in the nose or as she would call it 'her great beauty!!!' Good grief! Of all the people to smack in the nose it would have to be her. I feel terrible. What kind of boy punches a girl in the nose? I will feel guilty forever. I will never be able to forget it, and even if I could, Lucy would never let me forget it.

I was talking with Schroeder about his catching strategy for the team. It was a pretty important conversation – for me anyway – and I was really concentrating on what I was saying. Anyway, I kind of flung out my arm to show him what I meant about adding more reach, and there was Lucy. Or rather... there was Lucy's nose. I guess she'd come up to see what we were talking about, or at least to try and talk to her beloved Schroeder. She probably didn't expect to get clobbered in the face!

I have never punched a girl in the nose before. It's a terrible, awful thing to do. Boys should NEVER punch girls, even if they practically walk into their fists. I've never felt this guilty in all my life! My stomach is churning, and every time I close my eyes I see myself bopping her right in the nose. I can't stand it!

August 11th

I'm cured! Don't get me wrong, I wasn't right to hit Lucy. No boy should ever hit a girl, ever, in fact I guess no boy should be hitting anyone really. Anyway, I will never, ever do it again, especially after last night. I went to bed but didn't get any sleep. I was still awake when the sun came up. I couldn't stop playing the scene of me bopping her in the nose over and over in my mind. I felt like a monster. It was awful.

The only thing I knew for sure when I woke up this morning was that I couldn't fix this on my own. I needed professional help. The only place I could think of to go was the park. Lucy sometimes sets up a psychiatric booth there. People go to tell her their problems and then FOR FIVE CENTS, she tells them exactly what she thinks. I know, it sounds crazy that I'd ask Lucy for advice on how to feel better about hitting Lucy, but I was desperate so I thought her help might be worth the money.

✿✿✿

And boy was I right about it being worth it! It was like she knew exactly what I needed! As soon as I handed over my

PSYCHIATRIC HELP 5¢

THE DOCTOR IS [IN]

money and told her my problem, she looked me in the eye, leant across the booth and wopped me square in the nose, hard.

Boy did it hurt! In fact it still hurts. I'm not sure it isn't broken, but man was it worth it.

My stomach has stopped churning and now when I close my eyes I see Lucy's balled up fist flying toward my nose. From the look on her face, I think it probably made her feel a lot better, too. I just know I am going to sleep tonight. Well, I will as soon as my nose stops throbbing.

August 13th

Wow! It is HOT out there today! A few of us went to the lake to cool off but the water was almost as warm as the air. It was definitely too hot for Snoopy! I think the heat brought out some of his more basic dog instincts. Snoopy spends so much time either lazing around or doing people things that I forget that beagles were bred to be hunting dogs. Snoopy was on the hunt today. Sneaking and prowling, looking for some easy prey until he pounced ... on Linus! Linus did look like easy prey sitting there, clinging to his blanket. Snoopy caught Linus by surprise and bolted off with his blanket. Linus was mad, at first, but then he got even. I mean Snoopy is smart,

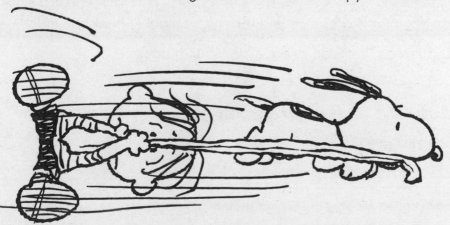

but Linus is smarter, or it least he was this time. He ran after Snoopy. He didn't have to go far before he found him. Snoopy had hidden underneath Linus' blanket. I guess he must have thought that as he couldn't see Linus, Linus couldn't see him! He can be so funny sometimes!

Linus, instead of grabbing his blanket and yelling at Snoopy, pretended he couldn't see him. Snoopy just stood there under the blanket in the hot, hot sun. Linus waited for a loooong time, as Snoopy got hotter and hotter. Eventually Snoopy got so hot that he gave up and threw the blanket back to Linus. Linus was just glad to have his blanket back.

I think this will make Snoopy think twice before messing with Linus again.

August 19th

Good grief! Girls! I just don't understand them! Peppermint Patty just went crazy at me. I mean one minute, she and I were sitting under a tree, talking like normal, ordinary people, and the next minute she is as mad as can be! She was literally yelling in my face, claiming that I said she had a big nose! I wasn't even talking about her. I mean, not really. And it wasn't even me who brought up her nose. She did! We were talking about love, in general. Not about anyone in particular, and definitely not about Peppermint Patty. I was confused then and I'm confused now. I just don't get it!

I should have known it was coming. Peppermint Patty said that she didn't understand love and could I explain it to her. How do you explain something like love? I think Patty has been a bit confused since that kid Floyd at camp called Marcie 'Lambcake'. I tried as best I could, but everything I said just seemed to make her mad! First of all I said love was that feeling I get when I see a cute girl walking by me. Patty wanted to know if the girl had to be cute, or if she could have freckles and a big nose? I guess she was right, in a way. I mean in movies, the girl is always cute, with great hair and a perfect nose, but so is the guy. I told her that I thought that in real life the girl could have freckles and a great big nose. Hah! To think that I thought this would reassure her, that it would let her know that I was sure someone was sure to fall in love with her one day. I thought it would make her happy. But all she heard was that I said she had a 'great big nose'. That's not what I meant at all. Sometimes you try to be the good guy and do the right thing but you end up being the bad guy anyway. I wish I'd never tried to explain love. Besides, it's not like I'm an expert.

I miss that Little Red-Haired Girl.

August 23rd

Back to school next week! Sally is really stressing out about it but I am not too upset to say goodbye to this summer. Let's face it. It hasn't been the best summer, what with the Little Red-Haired Girl leaving, camp and baseball and well ... you know ... everything. I will be taking some new classes with some new kids. I'm hopeful that a new school year will be a kind of fresh start!

Peppermint Patty isn't looking forward to it. Peppermint Patty loves the summer, getting to be outdoors all the time, playing sports, hanging out with her friends. She hates being cooped up in a classroom. She has a really tough time at the school she goes to with Marcie. She says she never understands what her teacher is talking about and that she gets everything wrong, no matter how hard she tries. I suggested that she ask her dad if she could transfer to my school, but she says she doesn't think it will make any difference.

August 25th

It happened! It finally happened! There was a gentle breeze when I woke up this morning so I decided to give the kite another try and it flew! It really flew! I was so happy! I was trying to savour the moment. I have waited for it for so long. It was beautiful! Linus was with me and I will be honest, he was kind of ruining it. Boy, can he overthink things. There I was, holding onto the reel and looking up at my kite, flying high in the sky above me, while he was asking me a lot of technical questions about the kind of line I was using on my reel. Was it 'monofilament' or do I prefer steel wire? I did my best to block him out. My kite was flying! What did it matter what I had on the reel? So I told him, it was string, and went back to marvelling at my beautiful kite. What a day! What a beautiful, beautiful day!

SEPTEMBER

September 5th

Peppermint Patty called after school. She said her first week back went even worse than she thought it was going to. She said that she just can't stand it anymore and that she had asked her dad if she can transfer to a fancy private school where they play lots of field hockey and she would get to wear a neat hockey uniform. Her dad agreed. He is out of

town again. I guess he feels kind of bad about being away all the time. Patty doesn't have a mum around either, so it must be hard. She and Marcie were going through brochures together tonight. She says they look AMAZING and was super excited about it. She said some of the schools even have Olympic-sized swimming pools and go on field trips to Europe! I'm kind of jealous.

I think Patty would do really well at a private school. Well, at sports anyway. It's funny, I can just see Peppermint Patty in a neat hockey uniform.

September 7th

Good grief! I came home from school today to find Peppermint Patty sitting in my yard and talking to Snoopy. It doesn't matter how hard I try, I cannot seem to get it through to her that Snoopy is a *dog!* I don't know what her problem is, but she seems convinced that he is a funny-looking kid with a big nose! Anyway, she had been talking to Snoopy and wouldn't you know it, Snoopy had found her a private school.

Peppermint Patty said all the ones she had looked at with Marcie were great, but that they all cost thousands of dollars. She didn't feel like she could ask her dad to pay that much money, when the school she went to with Marcie didn't cost anything. The school in the brochure Snoopy had given

her only cost twenty-five dollars! She loved the look of it. She
said all the students looked really happy and didn't have to
wear uniforms. Even better than that, she said that for some
reason, in the picture all the kids had their own pets!

I took a look at the
brochure and something
wasn't right. For a start
the school was called
'The Ace Obedience
School'! I tried to tell her

that I wasn't sure this school was the place for her, but she wouldn't listen to me. When Peppermint Patty sets her mind on something, there really is no arguing with her.

September 10th

I just cannot believe Snoopy sometimes! Peppermint Patty called after school tonight. Today was her first day at the 'Ace Obedience School'. She loves it and says that it has changed her whole life! She said she is doing really well already and that she finds her teacher really encouraging. She said every time she does something right (which she says is all the time) she gets a pat on the head and a treat! Her first class was on manners and they spent the whole time learning to sit. Her next class was learning to fetch! I can't believe she hasn't realized that she has enrolled in a dog-training school! I tried to tell Peppermint Patty that I didn't think the school was the right one for her, but she wouldn't listen to me! As soon as she got off the phone I went right outside to tell Snoopy that he needed to fix it. For some reason, Peppermint Patty listens to him and this is his fault. That beagle really drives me crazy sometimes.

<u>September 15th</u>

Peppermint Patty called again. She was really excited because she got her certificate today. She actually thinks she has graduated, for good, from a real school. It's unbelievable! She said she thinks she came top of the class because all the other students in her class were really lazy and made their pets do everything instead of performing the tasks themselves. Good grief! She is so proud of herself. She is going to be devastated when she finds out!

September 18th

Snoopy is really in trouble now! I don't know how, but he has managed to make a bad situation even worse! It turns out that Peppermint Patty's old school wasn't aware that she had enrolled in a 'new school' and were surprised to find out that she had 'graduated'. They said that in order for her to continue not to attend she needed to provide them with proof, not only that she had graduated, but also that she had done so from what they called a 'legitimate educational establishment'.

Peppermint Patty was really mad about this. She felt like the school were calling her a liar and that she would need a lawyer to help her sort it all out. As she didn't know a lawyer, she hired Snoopy! She actually took Snoopy, as her lawyer, down to the school along with her certificate. I can't imagine what she looked like in the principal's office, standing there with her dog-lawyer waiting for the principal to read over her certificate only for him to tell her that she had graduated from a school for dogs!

She said Snoopy made his getaway just before she found out and I haven't seen him since. I think he is really scared. He should be. I don't think I have ever seen Peppermint Patty this mad, and she can get really mad, but she is madder than I have ever seen her. She is determined too. That is one thing you can say about Peppermint Patty, she may not be the smartest kid, but when she sets her mind to something, she gets it done. She won't rest until she finds Snoopy and makes him pay, big time!

September 19th

I can't believe it! Snoopy is off the hook! Already! That beagle is so slippery sometimes, I'd swear he was part fish. I don't know how he does it!

Peppermint Patty came over looking for him. She was really angry and was acting kind of crazy – even crazier than usual. She looked everywhere for him but couldn't find him and then she climbed up on his doghouse to see into our neighbour's backyard. I told her I hadn't seen Snoopy all day and that I didn't see why he would hide in our neighbour's backyard. He never goes into our neighbour's backyard because of their mean cat. To give you an idea of how mean the cat is, his name is World War II, which is perhaps the meanest name you can give an animal, if you ask me. Peppermint Patty wouldn't listen (again) and said she was sure that that is exactly what Snoopy would want her to think. She saw World War II and got it into her head that it was Snoopy in a cat costume,

trying to hide from her. Seeing as she has believed Snoopy
was a big-nosed kid, a skating instructor and a qualified
lawyer, the idea of him being some kind of cat impersonator
isn't too ridiculous. She leapt over the fence and tried to beat
up the cat.

Peppermint Patty held her own for a while, she was really
angry and I think that really helped, but as I said, World War
II is the meanest cat you will ever meet. While they were
fighting, wouldn't you know it, Snoopy came home and wanted

to know what was going on? Peppermint Patty and World War II were making a lot of noise. I told him and I reminded him how it was all his fault.

To his credit, Snoopy looked like he felt really bad. We both watched for a while, willing Peppermint Patty to win (World War II has had this coming for a while), when Snoopy couldn't watch anymore. He leapt over the fence and joined in the fight. With Snoopy's help, Peppermint Patty was able to get the better of World War II and, even though they both got a lot of scratches and lost A LOT of hair, World War II limped away the loser.

Peppermint Patty was so happy to have beaten the cat and grateful to Snoopy for coming to her rescue, that she forgave him for the whole dog-training-school thing. I was tempted to remind her that she wouldn't have been fighting

World War II if it hadn't been for
Snoopy. I didn't tell her because I
was kind of proud of him. Snoopy
is terrified of World War II and
yet he faced up to him because, as
scared as he was, his friendship
with Peppermint Patty was more
important.

<u>September 22nd</u>

Walked over to see Peppermint Patty today. I wanted to check
she was okay about going back to school tomorrow. She had
hoped she might be able to enrol in one of the other private
schools she and Marcie had looked at, but she was too late.
As the school year has already started they told her that
she would have to wait and apply again next year. She wasn't
pleased but what else could she do? I would like to think that

this whole dog-training school incident might make her think twice before taking part in one of Snoopy's schemes, but I'm not altogether hopeful.

OCTOBER

October 2nd

I've been thinking. Baseball really didn't go so well for me this year, or last year, or the year before that! Every year, I blame myself, I blame the team, but maybe it is time that I started blaming the sport. I've always dreamed of becoming a pro ball player one day, but in a lot of ways it would be a relief just to shrug my shoulders and say, you know what? Maybe baseball just isn't for me.

I was thinking about what I could do instead. What do you think about football, Journal? I've played around with my it before, but maybe it is time I started to take it a bit more seriously. I know I'm not a big guy, so I might not be so good at tackling or taking other players down, but I could make a good kicker. I am going to take the ball out tomorrow and give it a try. To think, this could mean a fresh start in a new sport for me.

October 6th

Well I guess that's that – while Lucy is living in the neighbourhood, there will be no fresh start in a new sport for me. I took the ball out today to do a few practice kicks. You know, to warm myself up a bit, get myself used to the ball before maybe trying out for the school team, when who walked past my yard? Yep, you've guessed it. Lucy. She said she would hold the ball steady for me so I could concentrate on getting a good run at it. She seemed like she really wanted to help. She asked me to

look into her 'innocent eyes' and I swear, her eyes did look innocent. I don't know why I ever believe a word she says.

I took a run at the ball and had got up some good speed. I was determined. I was going to kick that football clear to the moon! Ha! Instead of kicking that darned football to the moon I ended up flat on my back, seeing stars. I can't stand it! She pulled

the ball away, just as I was about to kick it into orbit. Man, did it hurt!

October 16th

Good grief! It is over two weeks until Halloween and people have already started going crazy. 'What costume will you wear this year, Charlie Brown?' 'Where do you think you will go trick or treating, Charlie Brown?' 'Do you think you will get more treats than tricks this year, Charlie Brown? ... You do? ... HAHAHAHAHA!'

I wish it were a proper holiday, then we'd get some vacation days from school, and I'd be able to work on a really good costume.

I was going to joke with Linus about how crazy everyone was acting, when I remembered that Linus gets more excited about Halloween than anyone. According to Linus, Halloween is when 'The Great Pumpkin' rises out of the pumpkin patch with his bag of toys for all the good little children of the world. As far as I can tell, The Great Pumpkin is like Linus' Santa Claus. I have no idea where he got the idea from, but it doesn't matter how many people tell him he is crazy or laugh in his face or even how many times The Great Pumpkin fails to show up, Linus is convinced he is real.

October 19th

I went to the store with Linus today and he did not stop talking about The Great Pumpkin. He was very concerned that I hadn't sent The Great Pumpkin my Pumpkin List and he even tried to buy Pumpkin Cards at the store. He was really sad that they didn't have any.

Poor guy. I kind of feel sorry for him. He was like this last year and Lucy and I really ganged up on him. He was really depressed when The Great Pumpkin didn't show. I think I will go along with it this year. He is my best friend and it isn't like I have been invited to anyone's Halloween Party, again.

October 21st

Linus came over today so that we could write my letter to The Great Pumpkin together. I wrote a list of all the things I wanted for Christmas. I figured it wouldn't do any harm to start to think about what I wanted from Santa a bit earlier this year. This whole Great Pumpkin thing is a bit hard to get behind though. When I asked Linus where I needed to send it, he answered 'The "Great Pumpkin" Care of "The Pumpkin Patch."' Our mailman is going to think I have gone as crazy as Linus!

Well, I sent my letter. Linus says all I have to do now is wait. Good grief!

October 30th

Wow! Lucy is being even more difficult with Linus than usual. She just won't leave the whole Great Pumpkin thing alone. She is acting as though Linus believing in The Great Pumpkin is some kind of threat to Santa Claus. I mean, as if anything could threaten Santa Claus! Everyone knows that Santa is invincible. Any man capable of flying all around the world delivering toys to every good boy and girl in a single night could never be defeated by a half-man-half-squash mutant. That's just basic science.

I felt so bad for Linus that I agreed to go with him tomorrow night to the pumpkin patch and wait for The Great Pumpkin. It's funny, when someone you know believes in something as strongly as Linus believes in The Great Pumpkin, it's infectious, like the flu or some other disease. Don't get me wrong, I know the whole idea of The Great Pumpkin is crazy, but part of me is half expecting something to actually happen in the pumpkin patch tomorrow.

NOVEMBER

November 1st

Linus and I sat in that dumb pumpkin patch for hours. It was really cold and quiet. I asked Linus why he thought The Great Pumpkin would appear in this particular pumpkin patch rather than any of the others. According to Linus, he chose the patch we were in, because he believed that of all the pumpkin patches the one we were sitting in was the 'most sincere'. What does that even mean?

I tried to ask him how one pumpkin patch could be more sincere than another and what a pumpkin patch could do to make itself 'insincere', but I lost interest in what he was saying not long after he started talking.

We waited and waited in the cold until, all of sudden, from behind a bush we saw something. Linus was so shocked that he fainted, right there in the middle of the field. After all that it was just Snoopy! That crazy beagle. When Linus came round, he was expecting to see a pile of toys or some other sign that The Great Pumpkin had come. He was so disappointed when I told him.

I don't know what I was thinking. Waiting in a cold pumpkin patch all night for a half-pumpkin-half-man type creature that I knew did not exist. I like to think I did it because I was a good friend, but seeing how

depressed Linus was when he came over this afternoon, I don't see that I helped him one bit. He really believed in The Great Pumpkin and this has really shaken his confidence.

It's horrible when your confidence is shaken. I should know. It happens to me almost every week. I often wonder what it would be like never to lose confidence in myself, to be 100% sure that I was right 100% of the time, to be ... well ... I guess I would feel like Lucy. Ha! I'm 100% sure I wouldn't like that! Maybe I am better off just the way I am.

I gave Linus some chocolate and a pat on the back. It seemed to really cheer him up. I think I'd like it if someone gave me some chocolate and a pat on the back when my confidence was shaken. I sure would get to eat a lot of chocolate.

November 8th

Wow! Linus may have lost his confidence in The Great Pumpkin, but he sure hasn't lost confidence in himself. If

anything the Great-Pumpkin-Patch setback seems to have inspired him to take control of his life. He is writing a book all about his loss of faith and childhood innocence. He thinks he can turn his experiences into something that might help other kids. I think it's great, I just wish he wasn't planning to start on me!

November 9th

Linus came over today. Part of this whole wanting-to-take-control-of-his-life thing is him wanting to give up his blanket, once and for all. I honestly don't think I can go through this with him again. I think Linus must have sensed this, and that is why he wanted to talk to Snoopy and not to me. Linus gave Snoopy his blanket and told him that he wasn't to give it back to him no matter what. He told Snoopy that it didn't matter if he came to Snoopy, begging, pleading or even crying, Snoopy was not to give the blanket back to him.

Snoopy looked really excited. At first I was surprised. It's not like Snoopy to agree to do something to help someone else, and then I realized, it's not like Snoopy to agree to do something to help someone else … unless there is something in it for Snoopy!

I don't know what that devious beagle has in mind, but I can't imagine this is going to end well for Linus and I'm pretty sure that somehow, this is all going to end up being my fault. Good grief!

November 11th

Linus looks terrible. He came over to beg Snoopy for his blanket back. I was surprised it took him so long. He says that he hasn't slept in two days and he doesn't think he can live without it. Snoopy wasn't here, but I told Linus I would do everything I could to help him get it back.

⭐⭐⭐

I CANNOT believe that beagle! Don't get me wrong, that dog has let me down before, but this time I can't even look at him. Linus came back to ask for his blanket, only to find that his blanket was gone, for good! Snoopy had had it made into a pair of jackets for him and his bird friend Woodstock. There is no more blanket. Linus went crazy. Yelling at Snoopy and then yelling at me. He says it is my fault because Snoopy is my dog! I hate how Snoopy does these things but then gets off the hook just because he is a dog. Sometimes I really wish I was a dog.

It was really sad. Linus kept running after Snoopy trying to get a feel of his jacket, but Snoopy wouldn't let him get near it.

I feel so bad for him. It is partly his own fault for giving his blanket to Snoopy, but Snoopy is my dog. I know better than anyone what Snoopy is like. Linus is my best friend. I knew better than anyone that he would want that blanket back. I should have stopped Linus. I should have stopped Snoopy. I should stop *myself* admitting that actually those darn jackets looked really smart! *Auuugh!* There must be something I can do to make it right.

November 13th

Well you've really done it this time, Charlie Brown! You let your best friend down in the worst possible way. Linus had done it. He'd really done it. He'd given up his blanket and he was doing real good. He'd had a rough few days and for a while we all thought he was going crazy, but then he woke up one morning and realized that he was fine without it – his hands weren't shaking anymore, he wasn't sweating. Linus was sure that he could get through the day and all the days that followed without his blanket. He was so happy, at least that's what Lucy told me after I had, as she put it, 'ruined his life'.

I was just trying to make things right. Linus looked so bad when he left my house that I spent all day yesterday searching the local thrift stores for a blanket just like the one Snoopy had wrecked. I was so happy when I found one at the bottom of a fabric bin. It was EXACTLY the same. I thought Linus would be happy, too. I THOUGHT I WAS DOING THE RIGHT THING! I REALLY DID!

Linus was so mad. With me, with himself, with that replacement blanket. He really thought he had it licked this time. He really thought that he wouldn't have to be the only kid in school, the only kid on the baseball team, the only kid OUR AGE that still had a security blanket. It didn't matter that he still wanted his blanket, it didn't matter that he still needed it. The blanket was gone. He couldn't have it. He and the blanket were through and he was doing just fine until I went and dangled a new one, the exact same as the one he thought he had lost, right in front of his face. As soon as he saw it his face crumpled, he knew he wasn't strong enough to resist it, he snatched it from me. The poor guy. He sat there, clinging to that new blanket in despair and it was all my fault. I thought I was giving him what he wanted, but what he really wanted was to never see that darn blanket ever again. I thought I had been a real friend but now I'm not sure Linus will ever be able to look at me again. I

don't know if I will ever be able look at myself. Good grief!

November 20th

Feeling a bit down this morning, Journal. The year isn't turning out how I hoped it would. I really thought January would have been a fresh start for me, but it wasn't. In fact the whole year has been a series of 'starts' but none of them seem to have been very 'fresh' at all. I think I will go and see Lucy at her booth. She really helped me out last time. People say a problem shared is a problem halved. I think halving this problem is worth five cents of my allowance.

🐦🐦🐦

People don't know anything and neither does Lucy. A problem shared with her is a problem doubled – and she's put her prices up, too! I'm feeling even more depressed than I was this morning. Lucy said that there is no such thing as a 'fresh start,' especially not for me. She said that no matter what new thing I start, or new place visit, I'll always be the same old Charlie Brown. I tried to explain that the people would be new, that they might like me better ... you know ... the people might be more understanding? She said that although that was true, it would only be true until these new people got to know me. When I tried to argue with her, she told me my time was up and asked for my money. Good grief!

November 21st

I've decided (again) that Lucy doesn't know what she is talking about. There must be such a thing as a fresh start, even for me. I'm not going to be the same old Charlie Brown forever. Nobody stays the same forever! If we did, why does anyone go to school to learn new things? Why does anyone try to do anything at all? If there were no such things as fresh starts, why would anyone even get up in the morning? No. Lucy is wrong. She must be. Right, Journal?

DECEMBER

December 1st

I sat down with Sally today to write our letters
to Santa. Wow! For a little kid, Sally can be really
mature sometimes. There I was writing a list of
all the things I wanted this year. A new racing kite, some
oil for my baseball glove, a new journal – sorry, Journal, it
seems mean to talk about your replacement while I am still

writing in you, but you understand. You don't have
many pages left for me to write in and we are
about to start a new year. A new journal will be
a kind of fresh start ... I know you've heard it
all before. Good grief! Why do I even feel bad
about this?!

Anyway, there I was, writing a list of all
the stuff I wanted Santa to bring me (or
rather rewriting the list I wrote to The
Great Pumpkin), when I peeked over Sally's

shoulder to give me some ideas for what to get her this year. I couldn't believe what I read:

Dear Santa Claus,
Do not bring me any presents this year. I want my
Christmas to be one of peace and love, not greed.

She even told me she didn't want me to get her anything this year either! What kind of little sister doesn't want anything for Christmas from her brother? What kind of little kid

doesn't want anything for Christmas from Santa?! I wish I could be like that. I felt really guilty when I looked down at all the silly things on my list. I felt even worse when I mailed it.

December 6th

Everyone is saying that it is going to be a really cold winter this year. We've already had lots of snow. I don't know how Snoopy can stand sleeping outside. I really worry about him out there. He has his own doghouse and everything, but for some reason he won't sleep inside it. He always sleeps on the roof! I'm sure that one of these days I am going to go out

there and find him frozen solid with icicles hanging from his whiskers.

Tomorrow I am going to build him an igloo to see if he will sleep in that instead. I've heard that igloos can be really warm inside if you build them properly. I'm not sure if he will like it, but Snoopy is a weird dog, he likes anything that is a bit different.

December 7th

Wow! Building an igloo is really hard work. I was out there for hours and even though it was really, really cold, I was sweating! The igloo looks great. I am really pleased with it and Snoopy looked kind of pleased with it, too. Well, you know, he looked as pleased as he looks about anything that he can't eat. Perhaps I should have built it out of Girl Scout Cookies! I really hope he likes it. I hate to think of him all cold out there when I am all nice and warm in the house.

I'm going to take a look out the window and see if he is using it! I really hope he is! I wonder if it really is warm inside?

Well... at least he is using it, I suppose. I'd be more upset if he just ignored it after I spent all day working on it. He is just using it his own way, as Snoopy does with everything. He's sleeping on the igloo's roof. Good grief!

December 10th

I'm so excited! Linus and I signed up for the school ski trip! We get to stay at a real ski lodge and everything. I've never

really skied before. I hope we get a good instructor. Baseball wasn't so great for me this year and I don't think I can face trying football again for a while. Maybe this will be it! Maybe skiing will be my sport. I can't wait!

December 20th

What a week. I'm sorry that I left you behind,
Journal, but I don't think I would have been happy
for you to see me like that, again.

The week started off great. The ski lodge was
amazing, just like the ones you see in Christmas
movies! Our ski instructor was great, too. He was
the kind of teacher who is able to tell you what
you are doing wrong without making you feel stupid. I didn't
know that could really happen for people you know, that you
could try something new without feeling stupid right away. I
definitely didn't think it would ever happen for me.

I really was having a great time! That is until I
rode the ski lift. I was so excited! You could see
for miles! There I was, high above the mountain,
looking down at kids from all over the state, when I saw her ...

The Little Red-Haired Girl! It was really her! I could tell, just by watching her ski. She skied the same way she walked, like she didn't have a care in the world. Like she had no idea I even existed. Even from all the way up there on the ski lift, I was sure it was her.

I wanted to call out to her, to wave, to do something, anything. I wanted to do or say something to let her know that I was there, that I had seen her, that I was so sad after she had moved away, that I wished I had had the nerve to talk to her … but I just froze. High up on that ski lift, I just froze, I didn't wave, I didn't say anything. I just froze. There I was, with

that chance I had been hoping
for since the summer, how could I
be blowing it all over again? I felt
terrible. I didn't think things could
get any worse and then they did
– a lot worse. I fell.

I fell from the ski lift all the way
to the mountain and landed with a crunch. I fell, in front
of everyone, in front of The Little Red-Haired Girl. It was
horrible!

Linus skied over as soon as he saw and helped dig me out. I
thought he was going to think I was crazy, or that I had hit
my head badly when I fell. There I was sitting on a mountain,
miles away from home, covered in snow and yelling about a
girl that had moved away months ago. But he had seen her,
too! Worse than that, he had spoken to her and even worse
than that, he had spoken to her just before she got on the

bus to go home! I had missed her again. I can't stand it!

So, Journal, I am sorry for having left you behind, but I am sure you understand that it was for the best.

December 22nd

I'm trying not to get too overexcited about Christmas this year. Some of my friends seem to have the wrong idea about what Christmas is all about. I'm going to try and be more like my little sister. Sally doesn't want any presents this year, just peace and love. I want presents, but I don't want that to be all that Christmas is about. Most of my friends seem to think it is about writing long lists of things you want people to get you. I think this is really sad. Lucy says that I am only trying not to get too excited, because I know that if I did, I would only end up being as disappointed as I get the rest of the year. I guess there may be some truth in that. It's not like I have received any cards this year. Snoopy has had hundreds of cards. I wonder about that beagle sometimes, I wonder what he does that makes him so popular. I wish I knew. I'm going down to the mailbox, one more time, to see if there are any cards. I'm not sure I looked right at the back.

There was something tucked into the back of the mailbox. It was my letter to Santa! Sent back to me unopened. Good grief!

December 24th

Sally cracked! So much for wanting a Christmas of peace and love! She wants presents, lots and lots of presents! Thank goodness I got her something! I hope Santa takes pity on her and brings her something, too. I hope he takes pity on me and brings me something. I still don't know how he didn't get my letter! You really can't trust the mail sometimes.

December 25th

Happy Christmas, Journal! And
Happy Birthday! We have been
together for a whole year now
and you're nearly full. Guess what,
The Great Pumpkin must have
forwarded the letter I sent him to
Santa! I got everything on my list!
I even got a new journal – sorry again!.

I'd love to say that this year turned out to be exactly as I had
hoped when I started writing, but I can't. I never did properly
introduce myself to the Little Red-Haired Girl, the baseball
team didn't win the season. I did find out what it was like to
be Mr Popular when I was at camp, but it turns out being
popular isn't everything it is cracked up to be.

Thank you, Journal, for being with me this year. It might not have been the year I wanted or even expected, but it wasn't all bad. We learned a lot together this year, Journal. We learned a lot of things that I am not going to forget, ever!

Very important things I have learned this year:

* Lucy Van Pelt is tricky, even if she does have innocent eyes.

* A 'fresh start' isn't always that fresh. Try not to expect too much.

* If something seems too good to be true it's because Snoopy is trying to get me to buy him Girl Scout Cookies.

🐦 You cannot talk about love, especially to Peppermint Patty.

🐦 When flying a kite, it is important to stay positive but NOT to overthink it.

The Kite-Eating Tree does not remember a good deed.

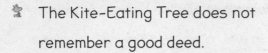

Marcie should not be trusted near a sewing machine.

Football is not my sport.

Baseball may not be my sport.

Either The Great Pumpkin is not real or there is a more 'sincere' pumpkin patch in which to wait for him.

When taking a friend to my dad's barber shop it is important to make clear whether said friend is a boy or a girl.

You should never punch a girl in the nose, even by accident.

🐾 When it comes to matters concerning Linus and his blanket, it is best not to get involved.

🐾 Snoopy is not well versed in matters of education or law and is not to be trusted.

🐾 World War II can be defeated if friends work together.

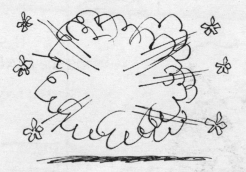

A rash on your face is not the worst thing to happen to you at camp but falling in love might be.

You really can't trust the mail sometimes.

U.S. MAIL

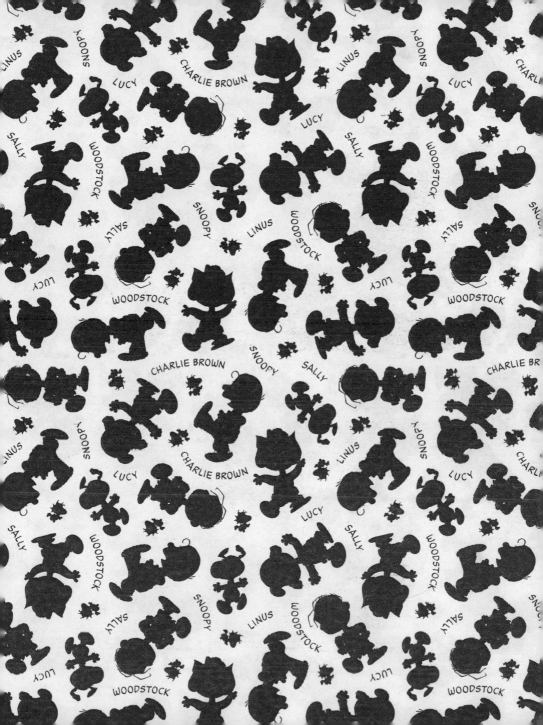

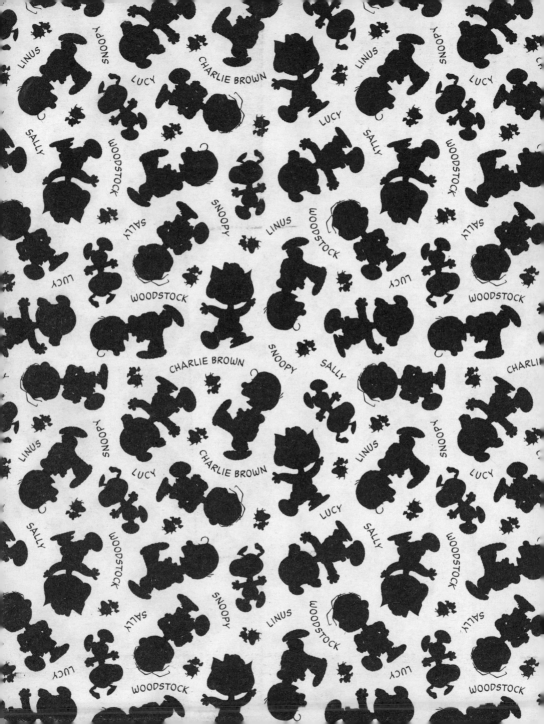